D1097967

2-
1c

Angelina Ballerina™

A Day at the Fair

Story adapted by Katharine Holabird
from the TV episode

Based on the classic picture books
by Katharine Holabird and Helen Craig

Grosset & Dunlap

GROSSET & DUNLAP
Published by the Penguin Group
Penguin Group (USA) Inc., 375 Hudson Street, New York, New York 10014, U.S.A.
Penguin Group (Canada), 90 Eglinton Avenue East, Suite 700, Toronto, Ontario,
Canada M4P 2Y3 (a division of Pearson Penguin Canada Inc.)
Penguin Books Ltd, 80 Strand, London WC2R 0RL, England
Penguin Ireland, 25 St Stephen's Green, Dublin 2, Ireland
(a division of Penguin Books Ltd)
Penguin Group (Australia), 250 Camberwell Road, Camberwell, Victoria 3124,
Australia (a division of Pearson Australia Group Pty Ltd)
Penguin Books India Pvt Ltd, 11 Community Centre,
Panchsheel Park, New Delhi - 110 017, India
Penguin Group (NZ), Cnr Airborne and Rosedale Roads, Albany, Auckland 1310,
New Zealand (a division of Pearson New Zealand Ltd)
Penguin Books (South Africa) (Pty) Ltd, 24 Sturdee Avenue, Rosebank,
Johannesburg 2196, South Africa

Penguin Books Ltd, Registered Offices:
80 Strand, London WC2R 0RL, England

Special markets ISBN 0-670-06117-4   10 9 8 7 6 5 4 3 2 1

"Excellent, darlinks!" said Miss Lilly at the end of the dance class.

Angelina and her friend Alice rushed to get changed.

"Just think, Alice," said Angelina. "In exactly one hour, you and I will be riding on the fastest, scariest roller coaster in all of Mouseland! Hurry up, William. We'll be late for the fair!"

Angelina rushed home and counted the money in her piggy bank. "Hooray!" she said. "Just enough for cotton candy!" Scooping up the coins, she ran to the door.

Unfortunately she bumped straight into Mrs. Mouseling and little cousin Henry.

"Excuse me, young lady," said her mother. "You promised to look after Henry today."

"But I'm going to the fair!" cried Angelina.

"Great!" said Henry. "I love fairs!"

Angelina sighed and, fixing a grin on her face, took him by the paw.

At the entrance to the fair, Angelina and Henry
bought their tickets with pocket money from Mrs.
Mouseling. Then they headed straight for the rides.

"Look at the merry-go-round, Angelina! I love
them. Don't you?" asked Henry.

"No, Henry," said Angelina sniffily. "Merry-go-
rounds are for babies."

"And there's a man selling balloons!" continued
Henry. "Can I have a blue one? Please?"

"No, you can't, Henry! I've only got enough
money left for cotton candy."

They walked across the noisy fairground until
Angelina found Alice and William.

The four mouselings rushed around the colorful fairground, looking at all the different rides, until at last they came to the ferris wheel. Henry could hardly see the top of it. It seemed like a very, very long way up. Angelina was so excited! She couldn't wait to jump on.

"I told you that I don't really like ferris wheels," whispered Henry timidly.

Angelina tried to reassure him. "Don't worry, Henry, they're not at all scary!" she said gently. "Trust me. You're going to love it!"

Henry reluctantly followed the others, and up they went, climbing higher and higher.

"Isn't this fun, Henry?" laughed Angelina.

But poor Henry wasn't having fun at all. In fact, he felt quite sick. "I want to get off!" he sobbed loudly.

Angelina was very embarrassed as the huge wheel came to a standstill and an attendant helped them step off the ride.

Henry held William's hand as the four friends lined up for the Haunted House. But Henry still wasn't happy.

"I told you, Angelina! I hate the dark!" he whimpered.

Angelina ignored poor Henry and dragged him inside. There were spooky noises, and it was almost pitch-black! Suddenly, Henry realized that he was no longer holding William's hand. He was all alone!

Henry walked bravely through the darkness, until
he thought he saw William. Henry reached out his
hand. But, oh no! It was a huge, hairy spider.
"Agghhhhh!" screamed Henry.

The lights went on, and Henry looked around him. The Haunted House didn't seem so scary anymore. He was very pleased to see Angelina and the others just up ahead.

"I'm scared of spiders," sniffled Henry.

He felt very shy as the attendant led them all out of the Haunted House. People were watching, and Angelina looked very cross. Alice and William wandered off, leaving her with Henry.

"Can I have a blue
balloon now?" Henry
asked Angelina shyly.
"And can I go on the
merry-go-round?"

Suddenly, Alice and
William rushed up.
"You should have come
with us, Angelina.
We've just been on the
swinging boat and the
helter-skelter. They
were fantastic!"

"It's just not fair,"
said Angelina.

"You have to come on the Loop-the-Loop roller coaster with us. You just HAVE to!" cried Alice.

"I don't like roller coasters," said Henry.

Angelina sighed.

Suddenly, a clown walked by. "Show starts in ten minutes!" he cried. "Wicky wacky fun for all ages!"

Angelina smiled. "I bet you like clown shows, don't you, Henry?" she said.

At last she was free! She left Henry at the clown
show, and soon she, Alice, and William were soaring
up high on the roller coaster. They loved it so much
that they rode on it SEVEN TIMES!

Henry, meanwhile, wasn't having much fun at the clown show. As his eyes wandered, he saw a big blue balloon float past. He just had to go and catch it!

A little while later, Angelina, Alice, and William arrived at the clown's tent to collect Henry. But Henry wasn't there.

"Henry?" whispered Angelina, her heart beating in her chest. "Where are you?"

The three friends ran through the crowds calling
Henry's name. They looked everywhere. Alice even
called up to the stilt walker because he could see
across the whole fairground. But nobody had seen
Henry.

At last they sat down on a bench. Alice tried to
comfort Angelina, and William offered her his
hankie to blow her nose. "What am I going to do?"
cried Angelina.

Suddenly, Angelina saw a blue balloon float past, with Henry running along behind, trying to catch it.

"Henry!" she cried. "Thank goodness!"

Angelina took Henry by the paw, and they set off through the crowds. Angelina even used her precious coins to buy him a big blue balloon.

"Look at the merry-go-round, Angelina!" cried Henry. "I love merry-go-rounds."

Angelina smiled as she helped Henry up onto his favorite ride. "I love merry-go-rounds, too," she said.